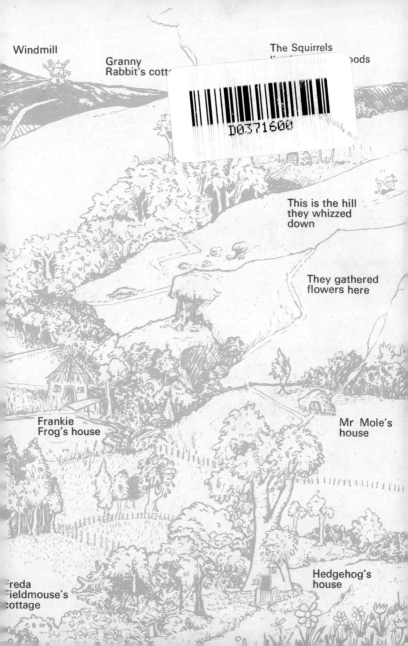

Windmill

Granny
Rabbit's cott[...]

The Squirrels
li[...] oods

This is the hill
they whizzed
down

They gathered
flowers here

Frankie
Frog's house

Mr Mole's
house

Freda
Fieldmouse's
cottage

Hedgehog's
house

# Tasseltip and the Boozle

Story by Sarah Cotton
Illustrations by
Ernest A. Aris and Roy Smith

*Based on the original characters
created by Dorothy Richards*

Ladybird Books Ltd  Loughborough  1975

# TASSELTIP AND THE BOOZLE

"Tum diddly tum," sang Tasseltip in his funny, squeaky voice. "Tum diddly tum," he sang loudly because he was feeling very happy.

It was warm and sunny, the best sort of day to be on holiday from school. He hadn't even minded when his mother had asked him to do some shopping for her.

He was still singing loudly as he skipped along the path towards the shop on the edge of the wood. Tossing his head in the air so that his cap would fly off and catching it on his floppy right ear was his favourite trick.

Letting his cap swing on his ear for a minute, he stopped singing and listened.

He could hear a strange thudding sound and, turning round, saw his friend Frankie Frog leaping towards him.

"Goodness me," he puffed, "I've been trying to catch you up for ages. What are you doing with your cap Tasseltip? – and what shall we do today?"

"Hello Frankie," replied Tasseltip. "It's my new trick, I'll show you."

Tasseltip and his friend sat down together on the grassy bank so that poor Frankie could get his breath back.

While he was waiting, Tasseltip tried to toss his cap in the air from a sitting down position. It wasn't as easy as he thought, even when Frankie threw it in the air for him. Finally, getting bored, he put his cap away in his pocket.

Frankie, now having recovered from the chase, suddenly asked Tasseltip, "Have you thought of what we can do today?"

"Well, I'm on my way to Mrs Hare's shop at Hedgerow Corner to do some shopping for my mother," he told Frankie.

"I've got to buy carrots and greens to make a salad. My mother said that when I had finished and brought them home I could do whatever I wanted for the rest of the day. I've got an idea . . . what about trying to find an adventure?"

"Ooh!" said Frankie enthusiastically. He had fully recovered by now.

"What a super idea. Come on!" And getting to his feet he leapt over Tasseltip and hurried off.

When they arrived at Mrs Hare's shop they discovered it was shut. 'Closed for breakfast', read the funny notice pinned on the door.

"Bother," said Tasseltip, "I do hope we won't have to wait long; I want to start our adventure."

He looked around and saw two other friends who also seemed to be waiting to go into the shop.

"Hello Friskie, Hello Susie," said Tasseltip. "Are you waiting to go into Mrs Hare's?"

"Hello Tasseltip, Hello Frankie," greeted the two squirrels together. Friskie was leaning against the shop door with his hands in his pockets. He was older than Susie and was always trying to look more grown up.

"We've been waiting for quite a long time," he told Tasseltip. "So I don't suppose Mrs Hare will be much longer."

Frankie was watching clever Susie. She had a long piece of ivy which she was playing with like a skipping rope, jumping over it again and again.

Tasseltip and Frankie each held an end of the 'rope' and swung it so that Susie could jump in the middle. Tasseltip had a turn, but he wasn't very good and fell over, making everyone laugh.

9

Mrs Hare finished her breakfast and opened up the shop. In went the two squirrels and Tasseltip and Frankie followed them. Friskie Squirrel did not have much to buy and soon it was Tasseltip's turn to be served.

He had remembered the shopping list but had quite forgotten to bring a basket. He handed Mrs Hare the list and she said, "I will lend you a basket and you can bring it back next time you come to the shop." She filled it with the things on his mother's list and handed it to Tasseltip. Thanking Mrs Hare he said goodbye and joined his friends who were waiting for him outside.

"I've got to take this home now," said Tasseltip, so they walked together up the lane chattering and laughing until it was time for the squirrels to say goodbye because they lived in a different part of the wood.

Tasseltip was still feeling cheerful so he said quickly to Frankie Frog, "Frankie, will you race me home?"

Frankie agreed and they both asked Friskie and Susie to wait a minute so that Friskie could be the starter.

Friskie agreed with Frankie Frog that as he was smaller than Tasseltip, he could have a start.

Off went Frankie leaping up the path until Tasseltip shouted, "Stop, stop, or you'll be home before the race is even started!"

Friskie, who was rather proud to have been asked to start the race, went up to where Frankie had stopped and made a mark to show where he could start from.

Then he went back and marked a place on the path for Tasseltip.

"I'm ready," shouted Frankie from his starting place.

"So am I," shouted back Tasseltip.

"Quiet please," said Friskie importantly, and he was just about to say, 'On your marks,' when Susie, who up till then had been very good, suddenly decided to be very naughty.

She began to run round and round Tasseltip!

"Susie, don't be silly," said Tasseltip, quite crossly. "You're in my way. Friskie will be saying 'go' any minute now and you're stopping me."

Of course that made Susie feel even naughtier and she ran twice as fast round Tasseltip until he began to feel quite dizzy.

"What are you two doing?" shouted Frankie. "Aren't we going to race?"

"Yes, but Susie is being a nuisance," cried Tasseltip.

"Susie, behave at once," ordered Friskie. "Or I'll . . ." But before he could finish what he was saying Susie had leapt high into the branches of a tree and was hidden by the thick leaves.

"On your marks," called Friskie and then Tasseltip got such a fright. Susie jumped right out of the tree on top of him so that they both fell over and all the shopping that was in the basket went everywhere.

They were all very angry with her but before they could recover, Susie got up and ran away as fast as she could.

"I'll deal with her later," said Friskie grimly.

When Tasseltip and Frankie Frog were back at their starting places Friskie called,

"Are you ready? On your marks, get set, go!"

They were off! Frankie was in the lead because he had a start and his short, stumpy legs were leaping along as fast as they could go. His green coat tails streamed behind him in the wind, and every so often he would turn his head for a brief look to see how far behind him Tasseltip was.

Slowly and gradually, and despite having to carry the heavy shopping basket, which he couldn't leave behind, Tasseltip drew nearer and nearer.

With his head triumphantly high, he sailed past Frankie Frog calling, "See you at home," as he went.

Frankie tried and tried stretching his legs as far as they would go, but it was no good. Tasseltip was soon out of sight and there was no catching him.

"Phew," said Tasseltip when he reached his garden gate. "Phew." Panting, he sat down to wait for his friend.

It had been an exciting race.

"Gosh that was exciting," said Frankie puffing and blowing. "You really did run very fast. You're the winner." He sat down beside Tasseltip.

After a minute or so Tasseltip picked up the basket and walked up the garden path to give it to his mother who was waiting at the door. She had made him a picnic lunch so that he wouldn't have to come home until tea time.

"Have a nice time, you two," called Mrs Rabbit as she waved goodbye, watching them walk up the lane.

As they wandered slowly along, wondering where exactly does one find an adventure, they saw what looked like an enormous stone in the middle of the path.

"Have you ever heard of a Boozle?" asked Tasseltip, watching Frankie playing at leap-frog over the stone.

"A what?" said Frankie, noticing that what appeared to be four legs and a head were coming out from underneath the stone.

"There's supposed to be a Boozle around somewhere in the wood," replied Tasseltip vaguely because he had just realised that the stone wasn't really a stone but Timothy Tortoise!

A rather cross Timothy Tortoise stood up in front of the two friends.

"I do not like young frogs playing leap-frog over me," he told Frankie sternly.

"I'm sorry," said Frankie, "I thought you were a stone."

"A stone? humph," snorted Timothy. "Humph, a stone indeed. Can't a fellow take a nap without young frogs playing leap-frog all over him?"

Tasseltip thought it might be better to try and change the subject, although Timothy had been taking a nap right in the middle of the path where anyone might have mistaken him for a large stone.

Remembering their adventure, Tasseltip decided that since Timothy was old and wise, he was just the person to ask about a Boozle.

"Timothy," he said, "have you ever seen a Boozle or know where one might live?"

But Timothy had already started to pull in his legs, and his head was fast disappearing when they heard him mumble.

"Ridiculous nonsense. Boozles ! Whatever next ?
Boozles indeed !" With that his head completely
disappeared.

It was quite obvious that Timothy was enjoying the warm sunshine and wasn't going to allow himself to be disturbed on any account.

The two friends decided they would go on with their search and leave him to his nap.

A little while later they passed a tree with nice straight branches, so Tasseltip stopped and, after pulling out his penknife from his pocket, he cut down two.

Then he stripped off the leaves carefully, and gave one of the branches to Frankie keeping the other for himself.

Whilst he tied his picnic lunch on to his stick so that he could carry it over his shoulder, Tasseltip said, "Sticks are very useful to hunters. We can prod bushes and part the leaves on trees and all sorts of things. Perhaps later we can float them down the stream."

"You never know," said Frankie. "They might even come in handy if we met a Boozle. I say, do you think Boozles live in trees?" he added, anxiously peering into the branches above them.

By this time the two friends had walked quite a long way. They'd come through part of the wood, then taken a path which led out of the trees and were now walking through tall, wavy grass.

Frankie Frog had been prodding the ground with the stick that Tasseltip had given him when suddenly he asked, "What exactly is a Boozle? I mean, how do we know when we've found one? If we are going to be hunters we've got to know what we are looking for."

"Well," said Tasseltip. "I'm not exactly sure myself. It's a sort of thing. It's probably got wings, which means it can fly. I heard that it lives in trees."

"I say," laughed Frankie, "it does seem silly to me, looking for something we've never seen." He started to giggle.

"I suppose it is," admitted Tasseltip, and he too began to giggle.

Soon they were laughing so much that they had to sit down. They rocked to and fro, holding their sides and leaning against each other for support.

Just as one decided to stop laughing, the other one laughed even more, and it was a long time before the silly pair became sensible again.

They rather enjoyed themselves though.

Eventually they both completely stopped giggling and laughing and wiped away the tears from their eyes where the laughter had made them water. When they had got their breath back, Tasseltip and Frankie stood up.

"Here you are, Frankie," said Tasseltip, handing him his stick.

He picked up his own, and the two set off again.

It wasn't long before they rounded a bend in the path and came to Mr Hedgehog's little cottage.

Old Mr Hedgehog was leaning over his garden gate, frowning to himself. He was a prickly old thing and no one liked him very much, but if you were polite to him, Mr Hedgehog could tell you all sorts of interesting things.

"Good morning, Mr Hedgehog," said Tasseltip very politely, as he stopped outside the gate.

"My friend Frankie Frog and I are on a very important adventure to hunt a Boozle, but we are not very sure what it looks like.

"Would you be kind enough to help us?"

Mr Spiney Hedgehog was in a particularly grumpy mood and he was made even grumpier by Tasseltip asking him silly questions.

Waving his paw in the air, he shouted, "Look here, you young scoundrels. Don't come bothering me, asking silly questions about Boozles. Boozles indeed! Whatever next? Be off with you before I catch you."

And he opened his gate and came scurrying out, still waving his paw in the air.

Luckily for the two friends he suddenly changed his mind. He quickly rolled up into a little ball and showed all his very prickly quills.

"Gosh, he was cross," said Frankie, who was a tiny bit frightened by Mr Hedgehog's behaviour.

"I think it's time we left," said Tasseltip. "Come on, Frankie."

They both hurried off as fast as they could without bothering to say goodbye to grumpy Mr Hedgehog. Not that it would have done much good. Curled up in a tight ball, Mr Hedgehog didn't look as if he would have heard them anyway.

"Prickly old thing," muttered Tasseltip, as they walked along swishing the air with their sticks and listening to the whooshing sounds they made. "If we turn down here, Frankie, to the right, we can walk along the bank of the stream."

"Good idea," said Frankie. "I could go for a swim. It's a heavenly day for a swim. Oh! Look, there's someone coming towards us."

It was a very frightened Freda Fieldmouse who was crying and wringing her hands.

"I'm so pleased to see a friendly kind face," she cried. "I've had the most terrible shock. Oh! It's been the worst day of my life."

"Calm down, calm down," said Tasseltip kindly. "Now, what on earth has happened to you?"

Before Tasseltip and Frankie could find out what was the matter with Freda, she slid to the ground and fainted. Poor Freda!

Tasseltip and Frankie looked at each other, then back down at Freda, wondering what to do.

"I know," shouted Tasseltip, who always shouted when he was excited. "We must let her have some air."

He rushed over to some bushes and picked the largest leaf he could find, and returned to Freda. Kneeling down beside her he immediately started to fan the air in front of her face by waving the big leaf backwards and forwards. Still Freda didn't move, not even by blinking half an eye.

Frankie had been thinking about swimming before they had met Freda and so had water very much on his mind.

"Tasseltip," he asked. "Would a drink of water help?"

"Good idea," said Tasseltip, "You go and fetch some and I will stay here with Freda."

So off went Frankie down to the stream, but he didn't have anything to put water in, so he came back to borrow Tasseltip's cap.

When it was full of water he carried it back to where poor Freda lay. "I don't think she can drink it when she's lying down like that," said Frankie. "I'm going to splash her face with it to wake her up."

So Frankie Frog gently splashed Freda's face with the water and she very soon opened first one eye then the other. Sitting up, she gasped, "What a fright I had, but I do feel better now."

Tasseltip and Frankie were pleased to see Freda looking better, but they still didn't know exactly what it was that had frightened her so much.

"It was Owl," said Freda, getting to her feet. Holding tightly onto the arms of her two friends she walked off down the bank of the stream.

"You see," explained Freda, "It's such a lovely day and I thought it would be nice to have a quiet rest. I found a big, tall tree with nice thick leaves on its branches and climbed up towards the top. I'd almost got as far as I wanted to, when who should be sitting there but Owl!

"I was so frightened at first that I couldn't move, and when I could, I didn't stop running, once I'd climbed down the tree, until I bumped into you two."

"Owl," exclaimed Frankie Frog, much alarmed. "I don't much like Owl. Shall we walk a little faster?"

"Don't worry, you two," said Tasseltip puffing out his chest and trying to look as if he wasn't standing on tiptoe. "I shall protect you from silly old Owl."

"Look," cried Frankie with glee. "Look, the stream. Doesn't the water look lovely?"

Quite forgetting all about Owl he ran to the water's edge and dipped in his toe.

No, it wasn't really cold at all!

Tasseltip looked round for a nice place where he and Freda could sit down, while Frankie, who'd stopped dancing and splashing at the water's edge, actually decided to go in. Leaving his clothes on the bank, he shouted, "Watch me!" In he jumped, making a big splash.

"I'm very much better now, Tasseltip," said Freda. "I think I'll go home where I will feel really safe. Thank you very much for looking after me, and will you thank Frankie for me when he stops swimming with his head under the water? I don't think he can hear me just now."

"Of course I will, Freda," said Tasseltip. "Goodbye. I hope we see each other soon."

"Goodbye," shouted Freda, waving as she walked away. And she waved her little white hanky until it was just a tiny white speck in the distance.

Tasseltip sat down once more on the bank, because Frankie was still swimming with his head under the water.

Tasseltip looked round for something to do and catching sight of some little coloured pebbles he started making a collection. When he had gathered enough he started throwing them into the water.

He wanted to see which stone made the loudest 'plop' sound. He was having such fun that he forgot Frankie was under the water until, instead of hearing a 'splosh' sound, he heard a funny croaking sound. A stone had hit Frankie Frog on the head!

"Croak . . . croak," spluttered Frankie, with his mouth full of water. Swallowing it, he said, "Tasseltip, you threw a pebble at me!"

"I'm so sorry, Frankie," said Tasseltip miserably. "Are you badly hurt?"

"No . . . watch me," said Frankie, and he dived straight back into the water again.

Tasseltip was relieved his friend wasn't hurt but thought he had better not throw any more pebbles.

Once again, Tasseltip was left with nothing to do. Frankie was still happily swimming, ducking and diving in the stream, and didn't seem likely to come out for some time.

Suddenly Tasseltip realised he was very hungry and remembering the picnic lunch his mother had given him, he untied the parcel from his stick.

Opening it up he saw delicious looking sandwiches. He closed his eyes and chose one, and after taking a very large bite he discovered it was his favourite, lettuce and watercress. "Mmmm, delicious," he mumbled with his mouth full.

It was just before he was about to eat his last sandwich that he heard a most peculiar sound coming from above him. He stopped munching and began to listen . . .

*The Boozle is waiting, the Boozle is watching,*
*His fingers are itching, his tummy is twitching.*
*With hunger and longing, for sandwiches gobbling.*
*The Boozle is watching, the Boozle is waiting!*

Tasseltip jumped up, dropping his sandwich, and looked all around him. There was no one there at all. What could it have been? Just then Frankie, who was by now a bit tired of swimming, climbed out of the water.

"What's the matter, Tasseltip?" asked Frankie, as he put on his bright green jacket and yellow trousers. "You look as if you have seen a ghost."

"I have," replied Tasseltip. "Well, not actually seen one, but I was sitting here eating my lunch when I heard the queerest thing. It was a message from the Boozle coming from the tree, I think."

Frankie roared with laughter. "You are as silly as Freda Fieldmouse."

"But I did hear something, Frankie," protested Tasseltip, who by now was quite pale. "Be quiet and let's listen."

So they stood very quietly and listened as hard as they could.

They couldn't hear anything except the birds chattering to each other and the rustle of the leaves on the trees swaying in the breeze.

Frankie started to laugh again. "I told you so. You were dreaming. I can't hear any strange, ghostly messages. There's no such thing as a Boozle. It was a dream."

Tasseltip wasn't convinced, and after looking all around him he picked up his stick and tried to reach into the tree behind him. Frankie helped too, but they were both too small and couldn't see anything.

"The message said he was hungry," said Tasseltip. "Let's leave this sandwich for him and go and hide.

We can come back later and see whether it's gone. I've lost my appetite now, anyway," he ended gloomily.

Picking up their sticks, off went the two friends.

"Let's hide here," said Tasseltip, pointing to a large clump of bushes.

Frankie agreed and, after making a little nest, he settled himself comfortably behind the largest bush. Soon there came a gentle 'Zzzzzz Zzzzzzz.'

"What's that?" shouted Tasseltip, leaping to his feet. Looking at Frankie he saw that he was fast asleep.

"Wake up, Frankie, you're not supposed to be sleeping now. We've got to listen in case we hear the Boozle."

Frankie yawned—and then yawned again.

"All right," he said, "I'm properly awake now. Let's go and find your sandwich, because if you've lost your appetite, I've found mine. I'm hungry."

So they both came out from behind the bushes and crept quietly towards the bank of the stream where Tasseltip had been sitting.

"You look, Frankie," said Tasseltip.

"No, you look," said Frankie.

"All right, we'll both look," replied Tasseltip, and they both peered over the top of the bank and, to their amazement, the sandwich had gone!

Before either of them could move they heard a loud snap of a twig breaking in the tree behind.

They were both so frightened that they fell over backwards into the stream with a loud 'splosh'!

Then they lay still for a moment, listening.

Tasseltip climbed out of the water and ran as fast as he could to hide in the bushes. Then he shook himself. He really was soaking wet. He was trying to dry his hands and face on his red spotted handkerchief when Frankie jumped through the grass towards him.

"Gosh Tasseltip," said Frankie, "you are wet. That was frightening. Do you think it was a Boozle?"

"It must have been," said Tasseltip. "Can you see or hear anything?" Frankie peered out from under the bush. "All clear," he whispered.

Very quietly, holding tightly onto their sticks, they crept towards the bank of the stream.

"Ha ha ha," laughed someone. "Oh, ha ha ha." To Tasseltip's and Frankie's surprise there was Robert Rat laughing so much he couldn't even say 'Hello'.

After a while he quietened down enough to blurt out, "Oh, you did look funny, both of you falling into the stream. Oh, ha ha ha." He began to laugh again. "Did the Boozle frighten you?"

"How did you know about the Boozle?" asked Tasseltip and Frankie in astonishment.

Robert Rat was really very mischievous. He stood with his hands on his hips, still roaring with laughter as if he'd never stop.

"Robert," said Tasseltip sternly, "what do you know about Boozles? I was eating my lunch when I heard a funny voice saying it was a Boozle, and because it was hungry, I had to leave it my sandwich."

Robert had started laughing again even before Tasseltip had finished talking.

"Oh, ha ha ha. You did look funny falling into the stream," he said. "I'll have to tell you, I suppose, to put you out of your misery. I was a bit bored and whenever I saw anybody, I'd pretend that there was a Boozle. It was fun to trick people. That's how you heard about it."

Tasseltip and Frankie looked at each other and then back at Robert.

"Well," said Tasseltip, a little disappointed that there wasn't a Boozle. "How do you explain the voice coming from above me, and who or what ate my sandwich? I did leave one, and now it's gone. How do you explain that? It can't all be a trick you made up."

Somebody began to giggle softly and, looking up, Tasseltip and Frankie saw Susie Squirrel climbing down the tree.

"We did play a good trick on you, Tasseltip," cried Susie, laughing at him. "I met Robert after I had run away from you all and we planned it. We have had such fun."

"Did you eat my sandwich then?" asked Tasseltip.

"Yes," replied Susie. "Playing tricks makes you very hungry."

Then Frankie and Tasseltip began to see the funny side of it and burst out laughing themselves. Very soon Robert Rat and Susie Squirrel joined in.

"You did bam-Boozle us," said Tasseltip. "Come on, let's go to my house and have some tea."

And the four friends headed for home.

The Squirrels lived in these woods

Mr Mole: Tradesmen's entrance

This is the hill they whizzed down

They gathered flowers here

The flower show was held in the Deep Wood

Mr Mole's house

WEASEL HOUSE

They looked for the 'Boozle' here

Hedgehog's house

The Voles lived in this old stump